The REBIRTH

SHEILA MATTHEWS

ISBN: 978-1-4669-4471-8 (sc)
ISBN: 978-1-4669-4470-1 (e)

Trafford rev. 07/02/2012

 www.trafford.com

North America & international
toll-free: 1 888 232 4444 (USA & Canada)
phone: 250 383 6864 ♦ fax: 812 355 4082

Contents

This book is dedicated to my son, Peter, who is a song and poetry writer. To my husband, I would like to thank for your support and believing in me. And to my daughter, Lauren, whose smile and bubbly personality always gave me the inspiration I needed to write and believe in myself.

Introduction

$\mathcal{T}$his is a novella. Names, characters, and places are all fictional. Any similarity to people—living or dead—places, or incidents in this story is strictly coincidental.

Imagine a world where humanity lived to their full potential. Scientists on earth have always said that we only use 10 percent of our brain's capacity. This story gives you an inside look of what it would be like to use your brain full potential and live to your full ability. I welcome you to the planet zippelli who now stands in the universe were earth use to be, on this planet, native's uses 100 percent of their brain's potential. Their lives have been achieved and perfected. Every event on this planet works harmoniously, everything on this land-dwelling has been well planned out for the good of all who lives there. There are no mistakes, no accidents, or illnesses.

viii   SHEILA MATTHEWS

Individuals are born healthy and live for an eternity. These fascinating creatures are a new creation of super natural beings. Each born with a different natural power, some are capable of transporting objects with their mind, some can see into the future. They can achieve or create anything they desire. They only experience joy; these natives have a system that works for all who live there.

This novella is for anyone who wants to imagine what their world would be like if it was perfect, take a tour inside a world where all its people function at their highest and full potential. How much could we evolve? What does the perfect version of you look like, how does one create a perfect life, if such a thing is even possible? All these questions are answered in this novella. Sara, a member of the planet, introduces you to this world. She takes you on a journey of how their world came to be, why everything works so well for her people, and the reason why their lives are picture-perfect.

The rebirth

*I*t's the end of the world, and you are okay. Imagine waking up and your life is exactly the way you dreamed it would be. Allow me to take you to a world where your life is just right. Envision waking up in your ideal house. Everything is precisely the way you desire it to be. You are with your perfect soul mate, and you belong to a great family. You exist in a place where each person wishes you well and treats you like royalty.

I would like to welcome you to planet Teleotia. This planet has a few similarities to planet Earth. At first glance everything seem to look the same, The trees and some of the animals here carry the same physical appearance but take a closer look you will find that they behave differently. Animals do not hunt or kill their own kind for dinner, they also feed from the tree of life. Apart from the fact that the entire planet operates differently. The individuals of this planet are called Teleiotians, which means "perfection." they possess supernatural abilities to move objects and create things out of their imaginations. These inhabitants are all wealthy due to their planet's vast natural resources and advance technologies. Teleiotians are proficient and highly competent beings. Their God like instinct is what guides their purposes and actions. Our entire civilization functions completely opposite to Earth. For tarters We have no need for government and we have no religion, yet the people of this planet are always happy happiness is a way of thinking some highly elevated people back on earth knew this. Happiness is our way of life. The word "sadness" is not known to them. There is no jealousy, everyone works together they have a common goal—to live freely and make the best of the life given to them. The Teleotians refer to one another other as kings and Queens. They are supernatural beings they have eternity. There are strict rules on this planet, which is why things run so smoothly. The rules apply to one and all. Every individual has an occupation, he or she works four hours a day, four days a week. Occupations are assigned according to the individual skills and supernatural talents.

My daily functions

Castle rock, located at the very top of old mount Ever Good morning Every soul is responsible to carry out a specific task these tasks are chosen by the individual. No one has the right to dictate to another being what their roles or what their functions Are to be. The work you do is totally up to you. The part you play is totally up to you. We all use our God-given talent and craft to help our community and our world. This process is called "talent sharing." We function as one; you can say our society is comparable to and ran like an Ant colony. Although we have different temperaments, we have a common purpose; we operate within that purpose—to live joyful a free in perfect harmony

My rebirth

I stand five feet five inches but always wished I was five feet seven inches. I had dreams of being a model but that dream was short-lived, I was not tall enough. I have always been called beautiful by my family and everyone I've ever met. I guess you can say I grew up to be pretty confident. I always knew I was born for greatness. I was always told by my single mom that I was meant to impact the world in some way. I knew my purpose was major, I always had a feeling that I had to use my life to help others in some way. Individuals are always drawn to me, being sympathetic and showing apathy are one of my personal strength. channeling the best out of people and encouraging friends are what I am known for. I always had the distinct feeling that I would have a major impact on the world—but not to save the world or rule the world, strangely enough That is exactly what ended being my destiny.

I am Queen Shelly. My name on this planet means "one who sees all good." I administer all moral practices on our planet. I am the law maker. I was not born on this planet per say; I was taken from Earth to rule this planet. I am all-knowing and all-powerful. My main responsibility is to enforce the laws and maintained the balance of this planet according to the instruction that was giving to me by God. As an adolescent on planet Earth, God visited me in my dreams every night for years. As I grew older, he visited me less and less. In my last encounter with God, as a child I was around fifteen years old, in my second year of high school. He appeared to me in a white robe, surrounded by a fluorescent white light that felt very comforting. God is at least five feet eleven inches tall, his hair is long and white and parted in the middle. He has broad shoulders and a great posture. He stands really straight and tall and speaks with confident. It was always very comforting to talk with him and to be in his company because of his calm and loving demeanor and his beautiful face.

I felt confident around him and knew exactly who I was meant to be in his presence. Something but for some reason I would quickly forget once I awoke. During our last encounter, God spoke to me. He told me to live a good life and be a role model to all who met me. During our conversation, he mentioned that he had a special mission for me, which he would reveal on his next visit on May 18, 2010. It was during that visit that he would show me in detail what my purpose was.

Having so many divine encounters stuck with me growing up. I was always nervous about breaking t he rules. I lived a pretty good life, for the most part. It wasn't easy for me to be godly, like he had asked me to be. I had a lot of peer pressure in high school and college. There was pressure from my high school friends to smoke cigarettes, which I tried once. I decided smoking was not for me when I nearly choked to death on my first puff. There was pressure to have sex and party while still in high school, and when I got to college there was pressure to try pot. Knowing God's eyes are always on you can put a damper on a young person's social and personal life. As a child, I was always good to my parents. They were always pleased with my decisions and the friends with whom I hung around. I had a B average in school and was somewhat popular.

However, I did cut a few classes during my times in high school—twice to attend a house party and the other few times was to the movies. I stopped attending these so called unsupervised house parties, after the last one ended in a big brawl between my boyfriend at the time and my arrogant ex-boyfriend. I wish I could say the fight was over me but it wasn't. I later found out that they lived in the same neighborhood and never really liked each other. My parents never found out about my playing hooky in school. They trusted me, for the most part.

I am pretty mild tempered, but then again I am a Taurus to the core. I was born on May 1, so every now and then the bull in me comes out. I go into a blind rage, where I lose total control of myself and scream my head off, which can be pretty scary. Like most Taurus's, I love very passionately, and I am also very loyal to my friends and family. I can cope with just about anything and fear nothing.

I have always been told I was beautiful, so yes, I am very confident. I am opinionated, outgoing, and can be very influential at times. I have a good heart and love to make people happy. On the flip side of that, I do not let other folks take advantage of me. My favorite saying "I am no one's doormat". Those who are close to me will agree with that statement "I always stand up for myself" and encourage others to do the same. I am very generous when it come to my friends, I wear my heart on my sleeve, yet I do not let others take my kindness for granted. The four words that best describe me are "influential," "affectionate," "sensual," and "persuasive."

I am not claiming to be perfect although everyone else seems to think that I have life all figured out, I really do not have all the answers. The truth is I am trying to figure life out for myself, I get butterflies in my stomach like everyone else, whenever I embark on some new task or face some of life challenges. The difference between me and some of my friends is that In do not let my challenges stop me. to me life is a game, I play to win, I use my setbacks as an opportunity to get creative. Life is all about your perception things are the way you choose to see them; I personally choose to see the bright side of everything. Maybe that's why God chose me for this assignment. He knew I would see this mission through to the end and would follow it through, he knew I would not back down until I reach my goal.

May 2010, ten years later, God appeared to me again in a dream all he said was "shelly who are the chosen one" than he vanished. I was then twenty-seven years old, married with two awesome children—a boy named Peter who is a whiz kid, and a stunning girl named Lauren who is more incredible than words can describe. There is, of course, the man of my dreams—my gorgeous husband, Kwame, who is brilliant and quite the character. Kwame has an amazing sense of humor; there has never been a doll moment in our marriage since we've been together. He is always optimistic, He's built like a quarterback with a heart of gold. Kwame is my soul mate. our relationship started in our senior year of high school. Our relationship started out as friends. We hung out and partied. Our relationship started on Valentine's party. We decided to attend together as friends, since neither one of us had dates. As the night progressed we started talking Like never before. May 2010, ten years later, God appeared to me again. I was twenty-seven years old married with two awesome children—a boy named Peter who is a whiz kid, and a stunning girl named Lauren who is more incredible than words can describe. There is, of course, the man of my dreams—my gorgeous husband, Kwame, who is a brilliant and quite the character. Kwame has an amazing sense of humor; there has never been a doll moment in our marriage since we've been together. He is always optimistic and love life's he is a kid at heart. He is built like a quarterback with a heart of gold. Kwame is my soul mate. We hooked up in our senior year of high school, he was prom king and I was prom queen. Our relationship started out as friends. We hung out and partied. Our relationship started on Valentine's party. We decided to attend together as friends, since neither one of us had dates. As the night progressed we started talking Like never before. The music made it a bit hard to hear ourselves talk, we than decided to take a short walk around the school to continue our conversation, and get to know each other better. He shared his dreams with me—made me laugh. It was during our little stroll I realized just how up standing and decent he was. I opened up to Kwame about some private things about my parents' splitting up, something I never really shared with anyone else. He helped me put the whole divorse in perspective, and reassured me that the divorce was not my fault. I felt a connection with him after our heart to heart. I think it was at that moment that I started falling for him, before heading back inside to join our friends, he looked at me and said "all that mathers is that both your parents still love you. you are not responsible for them splitting up, you should always remember that." now that I think of it those words made all the difference in my life. I become closer with both my parents. talking to Kwame made me feel so much better about everything.

After our little heart-to-heart, we went back inside to join our friends. We danced and all night. I found out that night Kwame was actualy a great dancer. When the party ended he drove me home—and walked me to my door. He said good buy than lean over and kissed me. The kiss was everything I taught it would be.-amazing. We were both taken by how much chemistry there was between us. I think we both fell for each other that night since or it could have been just me. He called me early the next morning and offered to pick me up for school. Of course I said yes, and well we've been inseparable ever since.

If anyone in this world knows me, it is my husband. He can always see right through me. He can somehow tell when something is not right with me whenever there's something worrying me he definitely knows. He is the only person in the world that I cannot tell a lie to, not even a white lie. He always know when I am keeping something from him. On our wedding day we vowed that we would always share everything with each other we promised to never keep secrets—. We share everything as far as I am cocern., Good or not. we are always truthful to each other and our children. That is the secret to our 10 year successful marriage.

There was something different about me. I never shared this with anyone, the truth is I knew a lot about people than I pretented to know. the reality is I had psychic abilities. I kept this secret to myself, because I didn't want anyone to think I was psycho—just psychic.

My best friend Murielle senced it, she once asked me "Shelly how is it that you can always tell how the people aound are feeling, and why is it that you somehow always know exactly what to say to make them feel better or encourage them." I answered "I guess you can say im psychic". she laughed thinking I was kidding around. I knew what advice to give to help others figure out solutions to solve their life's problems. So it goes without saying that my friends and family always came to me when they needed help or support. Murielle called me her therapist. She would kid around saying "can I come lay on your sofa for an hour, I have somethings to get off my chest." and after our heart to heart she would leave my house saying "send the bill to my house".

I would answer "call my office to schedule your next appointment session." we would both laugh at that joke everytime.

While we're on the subject of super natural powers I once manifested telekinesis. I was resting in bed one late night, after a long day of house chores and running erradns, I remember laying in my bed feeling exhausted. my bed room door was wide open, I needed to close it, but was feling a bit lazy. I shouted at my mom across the room "hey mom can you come and close my bed room door for me "my mom shouted back "shelly stop being lazy, get up and close it yourself." I was too comfortable under my covers so I waved my hand joking around to myself and ordered the door to close—and it did! I thought it was a fluke, so I tried it again, this time with the closet door in my room. When I did it a second time, I freaked out, to be sure I waved my hand and order the door to open and it did. I jumped out of bed ran into my moms bedroom and and slept with her that night, and for an entire month. I never used that power ever again. nor did I ever spoke to anyone about it. I had forgot all about that when I lived on Earth.

Reminising

My birthday had always been special to me. As an only child I got showered with presents from my favorite uncle, Rendy, and my aunt Josie for as long as I can remember. Cool things always happened to me on that day: I got my first job on my eighteenth birthday. I also found an envelope full of money—five thousand dollars—on my twenty-first birthday. My twenty-seventh birthday was the ultimate. On that day I had a gut feeling to buy a Quick Pick lottery ticket on my way to work, so I did. I played my birthday, my kids' birthdays, and my husband's birthday. On May 18, 2010, I went to work like any other day. Every one of my friends and family called me at work and on my cell phone to wish me a happy birthday. Some posted their birthday wishes to me on Facebook. I arrived home from work around 4:00 p.m. to find my husband and kids in the kitchen waiting for me with an ice cream cake. "surprise" They shouted as I walked in the kitchen. they sang me "Happy Birthday." It was really sweet. I went to bed earlier than usuall, it had to be around 7:00 p.m. when For some strange reason I felt very exhausted. I fell asleep as soon as my head touched the pillow. At around 11:00 p.m. I woke up to get a drink of water. I sat on the kitchen counter and glanced at my laptop with the lottery ticket next to it. I decided to quickly check the results online before heading back to bed. I grabbed my laptop and walked to the bedroom. I joked to myself, "What if I did win the entire jackpot? How phenomenal would that be?" I sat at the edge of my bed to logged on to the lottery's website to view the results for that night's winning numbers. I was hoping for a miracle, and a miracle I got! My jaw dropped, and my heart skipped a beat. I could not believe it. There they were, right before my eyes, all my numbers in the order I had picked them: 51821325445. I almost fell off the edge of the bed when I read them the second time. I must have read these numbers back to myself about fifty times to make sure they were correct.

I needed reassurance that I was reading the numbers right. I quickly shook my husband. I screamed with excitement "Honey, wake up. We are rich."

"What are you talking about?" my husband shouted back at me, half asleep. I showed him my lottery ticket while pointing to the numbers on the laptop. My husband flew out of the bed, turned on the side bed lights, and grabbed the ticket and the laptop from me. He read the numbers slowly the first time. Then he went faster and faster. We repeated these numbers back to ourselves and each other at least a dozen times. Then we both got quiet for a few second to let it all sink in. we turned around and looked at each other instantaneously than we both started screaming "we are rich, We are arich". The kids woke up and ran to our room, confused about why we were making so much noise. My daughter Lauren walked in the room and asked, "What is happening, Mommy?" she asked. Before I can answer my son peter walked inn half asleep walked inn and asked, Why are you and daddy making so much noise?" My husband quickly grabbed both kids in his arm and chanted to them, "We are rich, we are rich" he went on explaining to them that we had won the lottery. The kids were exited to know they could have anything they wanted at least that what they taught. We made a lot of noise that evening I'm surprised the neighbors never said anything about all the dancing they heard coming from our apartment that night. This was one of the happiest and memorable birthdays of my life. We spent the entire weekend planning how we were going to spend our new found fortunes. I felt like a kid again. The excitement I felt was overwhelming I felt alive, a feeling I haven't felt in a long time. Early Monday around 6 in the morning we all woke up, I got the kids dressed, we had breakfast as usual for the last time in that apartment. We kept the kids home from school. We got in our minivan than headed to the lottery office around eight oclock in the morning to claim our winnings. Peter started planning out his futures "hey mom once we get our money, I am buying a real car, an electronic guitar and video games for me and all my friends. Lauren "I want every Barbie, I want a doll house, and a bigger house with my own room" the kids went on this way trough the hole ride. They wanted furniture for their rooms, and last but not list a trip to Disney was at the very top of that list. I had so much fun listening to them go on and about what they wanted, I almost missed my exit. We drove for an hour, but it felt like only twenty minutes. Time does fly when you're having fun.

We left the lottery office at about half past noon we spent the entire morning there Feeling out paper work for our prizes, we had a session with an advisor who gave us advices about how to handle having such a large sum amount of money. We walked out with a check for a $108 million deposited is a secure account. The media had somehow heard about our winnings and were parked outside the office awaiting to get a glimpse of that person. They had received the news that there was a winner in their home town, they were parked outside the lottery office anticipating the winner to stroll out. They caught us by surprise as we walked out of the building. We were not expecting a parking lot occupied with cameras and broadcasters. not even the lottery office was also not aware they would be present. We became instant megastars. We decided the safest thing to do to ensure our families safety would be to spend the night at a seclusive hotel and hire round the clock security hotel until we figured out our new living arrangements. News had traveled rapidly, The following morning we found ourselves on the front page news. there was a picture of my husband living the lottery office on every Los Angeles newspaper. It was chaos, we were contacted by several television station offering us the opportunity on their show. we decided we would appear on one morning to share our stories. Shortly after the show aired we were contacted by a Hollywood producer who wanted to created a reality show about us. We signed up with them to produce one season.

The Second Visit

A month had passed, the media had setled down a bit, my family and I were now living in a much bigger house in Los Angeles, only a few miles away from our old community. We felt we needed to stay close to our old neighborhood, our entire family lived there we wanted to stay close by. We were now living in a $15 million family home with six bedrooms and ten bathrooms. We certainly did not need ten bathrooms, but we bought anyhow, the kids and I first visited the house we instantly fell in love with its charm. we decided to make an offer on the house after our first visit. The real estate agent we hired showed us at least 20 houses before we actually saw the house. It was love at first site for peter and lauren, I was sold on the house once I toured the house and took a look inside the master bedroom. The children begged and pleaded for us to purchase this house. They promised to be perfect little angels and never argue if we made an offer on the house.—had asked They were willing to do anything we asked. so we brought it-the exterior of our home had a striking resemblance to the white house, that is why the kids love it. My husband was sold on the man cave with the giant voice activated movie theater on the lower level of the house.

Life after the lottery

I was working with my producer Shannon on my reality show. I was no longer working as an editor at fashinista magazine. I was now the owner and CEO of very famous boutique called Forever Young. I had learned the inn and out of owning a retail store from working in the fashion industry, I knew a lot of major fashion industry players from working with so many designers, I had always dreamed of owning my own store as a way of making my mark in the fashion world. I had learned about the retail side of the fashion business and the different ways to advertise to created excitement to draw customers. I knew right away after winning the lottery that I had needed to start and run my own retail business. I saw a need in the fashion industry. Through my line of work I had met A lot of great new talented and brilliant designers who desperately needed a way to sell their products. These designers although very talented were having a hard time convincing big retailers to sell their brands. That's where I came in, I recruited the best of these unknown designers for my boutique. we carried great fashion pieces at prices that could not be beat. I name the company Forever young, it was an instant hit with the public. I had proven to myself that I really did understand the industry.

My husband convinced me one night at dinner "hey honey with so many new designers out there looking to get lines out there why not open a couple more stores." I ran the idea my by my advisors they agreed and gave me the green light. I started by opening a store in each major city in the world. That idea came from my son that same night peter "mom, I heard on the fashion channel that the best cities for fashion was newyork Chicago and California"-he was right. I opened my very first store on Union Square in New York City. The store opening was a success, it was an instant hit with shoppers of all ages, from adolescent to middle age women. Every fashion lover in New York flocked to our store. We created quite a buzz in the fashion industry. The mayor of New York and a few local celebrities showed up for the opening. My fame and industry connections made the company an instant success. The lines of folks that showed up for the opening attracted media attention, it made front page news, one local New York paper read, "Oops, she did it again. Another jackpot for Shelly peterson." We grossed a million dollars in sales in our first week—something I did not anticipate. I had to grow my company to keep up with demands. What started as dozen employees and a small cubicle space grew to over hundred emmployees and an entire 4 story building in downtown Los Angeles. Our profit was out of this world. We needed to ship products daily to keep up with the business . . . with the New York store being such a success, I followed my sons advice and opened up four aditioanl stores: in Los Angeles, Chicago, Paris, and London. Each opening become a red carpet event, with every fashion network and news media present. I new I had God's favor working for me. *Money Magazine* called me a "money magnet." It seemed everything I touched turned to gold. Forever Young was named best new company in one of the top wealth magazines. My life was one successful event after another. It was as if God himself was trying to send me a sign or maybe tell me something.

On June 18, I went to work, as usual. I got to my office at around eight in the morning, I skipped lunch, I had a photo shoot for a magazine about our new line for fall, and attended a board meeting with my staff. I was feeling a bit overwhelmed from being a CEO of a major company, and a mom, and wife. Work and life were really starting to get to me. I decided to take a mental health day. "Lakeishia" I called from my desk "please clear my schedules for the rest of the day. I am going home early, I will see you on Monday morning." left work early around three o'clock I called my best friend Murielle and invited hrt to lunch. I needed to talk to her about my hectic life and see if she would maybe consider woking for me. at dinner we talked and reminisced on the good old days, when we worked in the fashion industry. She started out as been my assistant, and we quickly became good friends. I was her maid of honor when she got married. I am also her son's Samuel godmother. After dinner I went home. I pulled up in the drive I stayed in the car and called my mom carol, I got to catch up with my mom and get the latest scoop about my family, Carole was the one who kept the family together, remembered everyone's birthday, and knew what was going on with everyone. I gave her the latest scoop on me, work, and her grandkids and their latest adventures and the silly things they did or said. She loved to hear about that, and I loved telling her about it. That was our little thing that we did each week. in return She would clue me inn on what the rest of the family was up to.

I got off the phone and and walked in the house around 8:00 p.m. The kids and my husband were eating cereal at the kitchen table. They were already in their pj's waiting for me to come home before they headed to bed. I grabbed a bowl of cereal and cold milk than sat down to eat. We sat at the table and talked about our day and the exciting things that happened to each one us. We talked for a whole hour. At nine p.m Kwame and I tucked the kids into bed. My husband headed to the living room to watch tv and unwind. I went to my bathroom and had me a nice relaxing bubble bath it was just what I needed to feel relaxed. I headed to bed afterwards. I fell asleep as shortly after getting into bed that evening. It was a liitle past ten thirty, I was exhausted. I fell into a deep peacefull sleep right away. around two in the morning I was awoken by a bright light in the room. At first I thought it was my husband getting ready to come into bed like always. I opened my eyes to tell him to turn the light off, and there he was—God, in all his glory—looking down at me, smiling. His face was lit up, as always. His presence felt so warm and comforting. He extended his hands toward mine, and he whispered, "Shelly, it's time. I have come to show you to your destiny." As I stood at my bed side, holding his hand. I sensed a sudden urge come over me, and felt the need to brace myself. That's when it dawned on me that I was embarking on something gigantic, and there was no going back.

The Transformation to a Goddess

God placed his arm around my shoulder and spoke, "Hear me carefully. You, my child, were created for this purpose and this purpose alone." I will equip you with powers that will allow you to control the moon, the stars, and everything on Earth. Whenever you speak, the world will obey." He placed his left hand on my head, instantaneously my hair grew from being shoulder length to waist length, my hair color was changed from black and wavy to honey blonde. shortly after I felt my body stretching. I grew from being five feet five, to five seven inches tall in an instant. My transformation din't stop there, my breasts got larger. Talk about your extreme makeover! God transformed me into the ultimate Barbie. I was very pleased with my new physical changes. The color of my eyes had changed, from dark brown to hazel, my skin, my hair and eyes were now glowing comparable to Gods. I felt a strange new feeling come over as the walls in my room started changing shapes and turned into a portal. The portal became so immense that it sucked in the entire room and then swallowed the whole world.

A New Awakening

*I*t took us a whole day to travel through the portal before reaching our destination. We must have been moving at twenty miles per hour through what seemed to be a tunnel of white light. At first I felt a little bit queasy. I have never time traveled before. This was a whole new experience to me. within a few minutes into our traveling, I began feeling fine, my stomach had settled down, I was able to feel relax, almost like being in my Mercedes. It was a smooth ride, but the landing was the oppositive, it was very rough. I would have appreciated a little warning, but God had prepared me for my mission. First, he explained my powers to me and how they worked. He demonstrated and I followed. I had the power to move space, time, and objects. I had healing powers and the power to recreate things as I saw fit. I always liked the idea of flying unicorns, so I decided to turn a horse into a unicorn. Then he explained in detail the reason I was chosen for the mission. I must have asked him about a million questions, and he answered them all. He assured me I would succeed at my mission. I felt calm nd confident at the end of our training. we portal back to earth. I fell asleep for the last three hours of our trip, it felt like I slept for eight hours.

What Is a Supreme Being?

God is very loving in every way, pretty soon the whole world would know of this truth. In the first part of the lesson during our trip it was explained to me why I was now a supreme being and the word "human" no longer applied to me. God spoke tome "Shelly you have been chosen to live on a new planet where everyone else will also be supreme. I am bringing you there as their leader to look after them and make sure they live righteously."

Then he sexplained "You and each person on planet Zapelli were created as supreme beings, free-spirited and perfectly capable of loving without prejudice. You were born with the power to choose and create all the things that can give you a great life. You were all created full of love, not hate; full of compassion, not envy; full of great ideas, not ignorance; full of light, not darkness." So were the beings on planet Earth, I added he answer "yes but somehow they became mere humans, unaware of their powers. They lived simple lives and have forgotten their purpose. Some of them behave like animals but with one clear difference—animals cannot write or speak." And then he shook his head and continued, "I am glad that all this stops right now. Living as mere humans will be a thing of the past". I asked him what will happen to every one on earth earth. He anwered "that is for me to know, all you need to know for right now is that you are now superior beings. A new day has dawned on you, on this new planet, and on its inhabitants, and now they can all live in perfect light."

Girl Power

My new assignment on Zapelli will be to remember what the old Earth was like and not allow Zapellians to become like the people on Earth.

I asked God to grant the power to see into the future—and he did. I turned to him "what would you like" he answerd, I continued "one more favor I wish from you father to carry through with this assignment. would you banish free will from Zapelli "why would I do such a thing" he answerd and I responded "I have never really been a fan of free will, or the story of adam and eve, man chances for survival seem to be doomed ever since he ate the apple. look at all the damage free will caused on Earth. Man chances for survival would be greater if they only had the will to chose good". As far as I was concerned, evil was the cause of all confusion and destruction, that it the outcome so call free will in the end it brought man and Earth crumbling to its knees.

I had this discussion with God a while back in one of our encounters on Earth. He asked me what I thought man's downfall was, and I told him free will. My wish was to banish free will and let man choose only good. Later on, God told me it was based on that answer that he decided to make me the leader of the new world.

The End of the World, the Birth of a New Species

When I awoke I become conscious of what had just happened, we had traveled to the future, to the year 2012. The month was December, the date was the twelfth, the day was Wednesday, and the location was New York City. This was where I witnessed the end and the beginning. This was how Earth became planet Zapelli, and this is how it all began.

Shock, amazement, bafflement—call it what you like, but that was the look on everyone's face that day. I remember it like it was yesterday. I woke up Wednesday morning at six. I was happy and content with myself. I took my morning coffee to the balcony to watch the sunrise. Los Angeles was really beautiful at this time of the year. I could see the entire city from up there. I would be heading to New York in two hours. My life had become a roller-coaster ride ever since I won the lottery. I was a $108 million richer. I had more money than I had ever dreamed I was a business owner and now I was in the prodcess of shooting a reality show. Soon this house would be filled with camera crews for my new reality show. I was now seeing the signs that God warned me about. The end was near, and I knew it. My lottery story, my business ventures could all be found on the internet and heard on the media. The whole world knew who I was. My rags-to-riches story was about to take a turn for the worse. As much as I was scared to admit it, I could no longer try to put off the inevitable. It was 2012. The world was ending on December 12. The signs were everywhere, but only I knew what they meant. My hair was changing, and I was transforming even more. I looked younger, I was stronger, and I could predict events in my friends' and family members' lives. My transformation was very exiting, the media went crazy, they were reporting that I was obssessed with plastic surgery. My publicist had traveling more and attending award shows and industry parties, as a way to promote my reality show. I become more outgoing and out spoken than before I was before my transformation. I felt like a new person I guess in a sense I was, I felt invinsible and it showed.

Secret Revealed

My husband, Kwame, was wrestling with emotional turmoil. For months he had noticed changes in my physical appearance that he could not explain. I wondered if ever thought he might have been going crazy. A week into my physical changes we were out having brunch. He mentioned to me that he wanted to see a therapist because he thought being rich was giving him anxiety. He had been having trouble sleeping since my physical changes had occurred. He thought being wealthy was making him paranoid. He was tempted to see a therapist and also wanted to confront me, but he didn't know how to do it.

As he analyzed and planned to confront me, he gathered evidence that I was a different person. Fear was setting in, yet he avoided confrontation. Kwame was my first love. We'd been married ten years. We had two kids, Lauren and Peter. Besides my mother, no one knew me better than Kwame. He mentioned that his shy and conservative wife was now the life of the party. I seemed to have grown two inches taller and two breast sizes larger, with no scars on my body.

My mind was spinning out of control. How was anyone supposed to react to such news?

I worried revealing myself to Kwame, I was terrified that he might call the authorities. I was freaking out at the thought of how much conflict all this might cause. I sat across from Kwame at the breakfast table on New Year's Day and fearfully told him my big secret. I blurted out, "I was sent to save the world from the apocalypse." I revealed to him that I was the reason the world would end. And told him what conspired with my encounters wih God. The approach had reaction to the news was shocking to me.

The following morning the camera crew arrived at The house to start shooting, with my assistant lakeisha, I will be followed for the next three months. I got dressed, ate breakfast With the cameras around. December 12, 2012 the day the world would end. we all letft the house my husband and I we headed to the airport. we boarded a private jet to New York City with the camera crew on board. This was the begening of the end. I wasn't sure if anyone one on the crew noticed the changes in my features. I was pretty sure someone would made mention of it if they thought I had something else going on with me. However, everyone did comment on my skin. My hair stylist, Keisha, commented that my skin was glowing. My husband thought I looked radiant, but than again he always gave me great compliments.

It was ten o'clock in the morning when I arrived in New York. I made it to my hotel from the airport in less than half an hour with no traffic. So far this was starting out to be a great day, even tough things would soon change, I thought to myself. I had a flashback of my neighborhood in Brooklyn. I really didn't miss that place at all. For ten years I lived in a broken-down apartment in Brooklyn. My neighbors were nice, and they loved Lauren—that was for sure. Now there I was, a few years later, shooting a reality TV show—to top it all of I was a millionaire.

After checking in to my hotel room and settling down, I called home to let the kids know that I had landed in New York okay. the crew consisted of Shannon the producer, Carlos the camara man Sammy carlos assistant, and lakeisha my assistant. Later that evening, we boarded a limo and headed out to shoot a scene of me and my husband shopping and dinning the most exclusives stores and restaurant on Fifth Avenue. "I can see it now," I said to my producer, Shannon, "once this show hits the airwaves, I will be a household name name." I stepped out of the limo on Fifth Avenue in Manhattan, I stood at the entrance of the Gucci store, as Carlos started filming I felt nervy. The event was getting closer. We were attracting a lot of attention from folks walking by, we kept having to stop, I had a few fans requesting to take pictures with me and requesting my autograph.

Keisha and Carlos followed me into the Gucci store. *This is all for show*, I thought would have rathered spend my day shopping at Zara, but instead we went to Bergdorf and Tiffanys, as this would bring better ratings. Shannon believed it was all about ratings these days. I turned to my husband and joke in a Jamaican accent "little do they know the ratings will shoot of the air waves once they shoot what will soon to come" my husband laughed. As we drove to time square we discussed our next stop, I glanced at my watch. It was ten minutes to noon, when I stepped out the car, it was only eight fourty five in Los Angeles and eleven fourty five in NY time. I thought to myself, *My god, this is the longest morning of my life.* I guess had spoken too soon. I looked up at the sky, and this strange feeling came over me. I braced myself, for something big was about to happen. As I looked up at the sky I noticed the most bizarre and amazing thing I had ever seen in my entire life. About a million stars filled the sky. I pointed to the sky and yelled to my hair stylist, "Hey, Keisha, look!"

"Are you filming this?" I asked Carlos.

He looked up and asked, "What is happening? Why is the moon so bright?" New Yorkers passing by noticed me. I could tell They were tempted to run to me. I had to use telekinesis to keep them away. The event had starded it was show time. I stood in the middle of time square frozen in place unable to move. At eleven fifty seven am all the traffic lights in manhattan started malfunctioning. I used my powers to push the cars back. I extending my arms outward to stop them. Turning the car batteries off to avoid chahos, a cab driver jumped out of his car yelling for help. There was a pregnant passenger in labor in his car. Unshakable my husband Kwame rose to the occasion, he walked towards the cab driver and attempt to keep the mother-to-be calm. the mother gives birth to a baby girl. The baby needed help. She was not breathing. still frozen in place I extanded my arms toward the baby, I tried using my powers in an attempt to resuscitate her. I was distracted that I almost didn't notice that the commit headed towards earth had collided into the sun causing an immense ball of fire heading towards time square. I retorted by extending my arms towards the ball of fire and absorbed its power. I had captured and absorbed all of the sun energy. the people cheared when they noticed what had just taken place. I had to focus on my assignment. the first part of my mission was to stop the commit from reaching earth. I had to absorb all the sun's energy or the planets would combust into flames. A sacrifice had to be made at that moment. I had to quickly decide to save either the baby or the world. I Was heart broken by this, I could not hold back my emotions. Tears fell down my face as I pulled my energy away from the baby to refocus myself. The sun quickly turned to ash, and the planet went into total darkness. I spoke the message, "Let there be light." Kwame gave the fragile newborn artificial respiration. She began to cry, the world was still in complete darkness. Everyone paused and stare at me awaiting to witness my next move. The energy of the sun had transformed me into a bolt of lightning. Everyone was now aware of what was happening because someone shouted oh my Goodness, I think this is the end of the world. It looked like I was about to blow and take the whole city down with me. Kwame attempted to aproach me in order to comfort me, he was knocked unconscious by a bolt of lightning when he tried touching me.

I reacted with a wave of both my hands and shot out two bolts of fire, barely missing the pedestrians and the SWAT team. Pandemonium set in on the streets of Manhattan as people started to run for cover. The army general ordered to shoot me down. Kwame somehow managed to regain consciousness. He realized what was happening. He became tormented with worry. He ran and stood in front of me to shield me. He faced the fact that he might have to die to save me. I was unable to help, I could not move from my spot. There was a force holding me in position. It was like I was glued to the floor. I was frozen in place. I needed to remain in position until light was restored on the planet.

As the moon slowly appeared where the sun stood before it burst into ashes. The SWAT team got ready to shoot a rocket launcher at me. Pedestrians and bystanders were touched by Kwame's bravery. He shouted, "please stop she is trying to save you people! What are you doing?" Bystanders ran to his support and stood in front of me. They joined in uniformed and screamed, "Let her finish what she started!"

Kwame saw the world in a new light and felt he had a new reason to live—if only he could survive this day.

There was a final showdown between the New Yorkers and the authorities. The opinion on the streets was divided. Half of the people were screaming, "Shoot her," while the other half was screaming, "Leave her alone. Let her finish what she started!" these innocent people were putting their lives in jeapordy to save this person who had just saved their lives. The police the army and I at this moment were trying to keep the citizens of New York safe from each other. It looked like a sacrifice had to be made. Some people might have to die for this day to come to an end.

The people of New York and the army officials held my life in their hands. The only way I could save the world was to break the one forbidden rule. I had to go against everything I believed and seriously injure, or perhaps kill, someone. Kwame looked at me, and I saw the acceptance in his eyes. He said to me, "I love you for the person that you are. Whatever decision you make, I am by your side to live or die." Kwame's unconditional love and acceptance gave me strength, and I did the only thing I could do. With my power I repelled the police out of the roket launcher surfing above me. I threw them on top of a building. I turned the helicopters to ashes to avoid killing pedestrians on the ground. Kwame gets knocked out by a pedestrian that came charging at him through the crowd. A fight breaks out between the two apposing sides.

The moon reached its position, then like a bolt of lightning the fire I had absorbed from the sun escaped out of my body like a bolt of lightning. The fire escaped from my eyes and hands charging the moon with new energy. The moon transformed becoming brighter than the sun, illuminating the street like never before. The transparent light, coming from the sun's rays, shone and reflected on the street pavements like gold. A new world was born.

I regained my body and the crowed ran towards me thanking me with embrace. every one cheered. I started looking for kwame through the crowd. For too heart-wrenching minutes, I didn't know if Kwame was alive. Finally, we were reunited, and he assured me his wound was minor. I touched him realizing I still had my powers, I healed him back to perfect health. The people again rejoiced, all this was caught on film. The whole world had just witnessed their first miracle: the new Earth.

There were a million stars in the sky at that moment, shining like diamonds and spinning around like crystal balls. The Earth was transforming right before our eyes, and by now everyone knew what was happening. Out of the blue the sun started to set it was now 1pm.

As I stood there with my mouth open, I kept gazing at the stars, mesmerized by what was taking place right before my eyes. More folks started gathering around me. Everyone were getting out of their cars to witness this phenomenon. The world stood still at that very moment. For once New Yorkers were standing still. All was quiet. As the sun set, A new moon appeaed, the moon got brighter and brighter.

The Earth began shaking and the wind started blowing, but no one panicked. Everyone was calm and seemed to actually enjoy all this. People were gathering around me. They sensed I was the one causing all this. A child asked me "miss shelly are the one causing all this. I answered, "No, honey, you are witnessing a real miracle."

"This day better not get any weirder," I whispered to Keisha. who came to embrace me. Again I spoke too soon. A man who had both legs amputated and was in a wheelchair started screaming, "What is happening?" He grabbed my hands and would not let go. What happened next was the beginning of one of the many weird things that were to follow. The man in the wheelchair, who later told me his name was Patrick, experienced his legs growing back from the kneecaps. In seconds he had two legs and was standing up.

"How did you do that?" the little boy asked me.

I quickly replied, "Honey, this is not my doing."

Across the street another man with one arm started screaming. His arm was growing back. People were taking their glasses off, because they were seeing clearly. Older people were becoming younger by the second. Carlos's receding hairline had grown back to a full head of hair. He was a forty-year-old man a minute ago, but now he looked no more than twenty-five. It wasn't just him. Everyone over forty looked twenty-five. I reached into my pocket for a small mirror and showed him his new look. Tears of joy were flowing down his cheeks. He smiled at me and said, "I knew today was going to be a life-changing moment for me." He kept filming all the miracles happening around us. People were laughing, jumping, and hugging each other. I had never seen

New Yorkers so ecstatic. They were friendlier than ever. The whole street was celebrating, and it was only 3:00 p.m. The sun had completely set. No one was budging or trying to go home. Everyone stood there, enjoying themselves. All you could see for miles and miles were millions of stars and a bright, beautiful moon in the sky that lit up the whole street.

Explanation

So there is the answer, people. The end of the world is December 12, 2012.

It seems this phenomenon had occurred all over the world. Every media and network were reporting the same event. they were all talking about the same thing they trying to come up with an explanation for all this and seeking to make sense of all this.

What a day it was, I was glad it was over. My mission was over I had succeed in saving the world. I was ready to go back home to be with my kids and family. I boarded the private plane back to Los Angeles the following day. When I arrived home in L.A, I found the entire media parked outside our home. We were reunited with our children. Hey were extatic to see us Kwame and I. Lauren mentioned to me, "Mom, you and dad are heroes."

This new world learned the had a new hero capable to heal them and keep them safe.

Kwame learned that courage has many faces, and I learned that I am a strong, and brave. Together we discovered that some battles are worth fighting—even worth dying—for. Our experience had made our union even stronger.

My entire family was gathered in the living room, watching us on TV, when I walked into the room. The first person that I noticed was my mom, Carol. Then there was my mother-in-law, Pat; my auntie, Marie; my niece, Renee; and my uncle, Rendy. Twenty some members of my immediate family of mine and my husband's family were all gathered in our home. Thank God we hsd all these extra rooms restrooms availabke in the house. I guess they finally came in handy.

After I won the lottery, I moved all my close family and friends to live nearby. We all lived about ten to fifteen minutes from each other. I was so glad to know I did not have to make twenty-plus phone calls that day, everyone I cared about was right now under one roof.

While my day seemed to get longer by the second, my family was enjoying themselves. Every one of them had experienced some extreme makeovers. Everyone looked twenty-five years old. My mom looked like my twin sister, and I almost did not recognize my mother-in-law. It seemed the kids did not change much. The news reported only adults over forty and people with illnesses were affected by these changes. The deaf could hear, the blind could see, the sick were healed, and everyone who wore glasses did not need them anymore. The entire planet had twenty-twenty vision. Everyone was happy with themselves.

Later that evening, with the TV now turned off, everyone in my family got together at the dinner table to enjoy a nice all-American meal. We pulled three tables together so everyone would fit. We talked and laughed and joked until the wee hours of the morning. Finally everyone gathered in groups of four and shared a room in the house. I slept in my room with my husband and two kids, and the rest of my family figured out their sleeping arrangements separately. My husband, the kids, and I fell asleep, gazing at the stars and the moon through the ceiling's skylight. By 11:00pm. everyone was fast asleep, and the house was completely quiet.

World Amnesia: The Morning After

At about eight o'clock in the morning I awakened feeling well rested, more alive, and stronger than I had ever felt. I grabbed a cup of tea to my room's balcony.

The sun had completely risen, and the entire planet now looked different. I had had the weirdest of being in the future that night. My wishes seemed to have all come true. The season had changed, and the trees had changed colors overnight. We went from summer to fall in less than two hours. Although everyone seemed to look the same and the physical changes were permanent, they had no memory of how they acquired their new look or what happened to the whole world the day before. Unlike everyone else, my husband and kids remembered small pieces of the day, but no one was talking about it. The news was reporting the weather, as if the entire planet had amnesia. Everyone had only pleasant memories of their childhood and their lives. No one remembered anything sad or understood me when I used the word "sad." They were using strange new words that I had never heard of before. It took me a whole week to figure out Zapelli was the planet on which we were living. We were all living in a different world, but only I knew how we got there. Earth had completely vanished from existence, and a new world had formed in twelve hours.

The End

I would like to thank my husband, Dion Matthews, and son, Peter Matthews, for their support in helping me write this novella. Their input gave me confidence, and their eagerness to reach each chapter as I completed it gave me support. They gave me the motivation I needed to make this story come to life.

About the Author

Sheila Matthews has always loved writing. Storytelling has always been her passion Fueled by a vivid imagination, whether it is writing poetry, short stories, or novels. She likes to tell stories that are out of this world. She has always been inspired by writing. Sheila has said that her inspiration for writing is "the power of words and its ability to transform and shape the world around us". As a child Sheila loved to write poetry. Her love for writing started around 13 when her favorite uncle commented on how a Christmas card she wrote him brought him to tears. She has been writing ever since. "I can't remember a time when I didn't have a pen or a pencil in my hand, writing has always been a part of who I am" she says....Sheila wrote her first book at the age of 19. Following that turning point in her life, she hasn't ceased writing. Sheila does a lot of recreational writing as well, including poetry songwriting, and short stories for young adults.

She is also a philanthropist, the CEO of a non-profit providing food, clothing and educational supplies for families in need.